IF ONCE YOU HAVE SLEPT ON AN
ISLAND

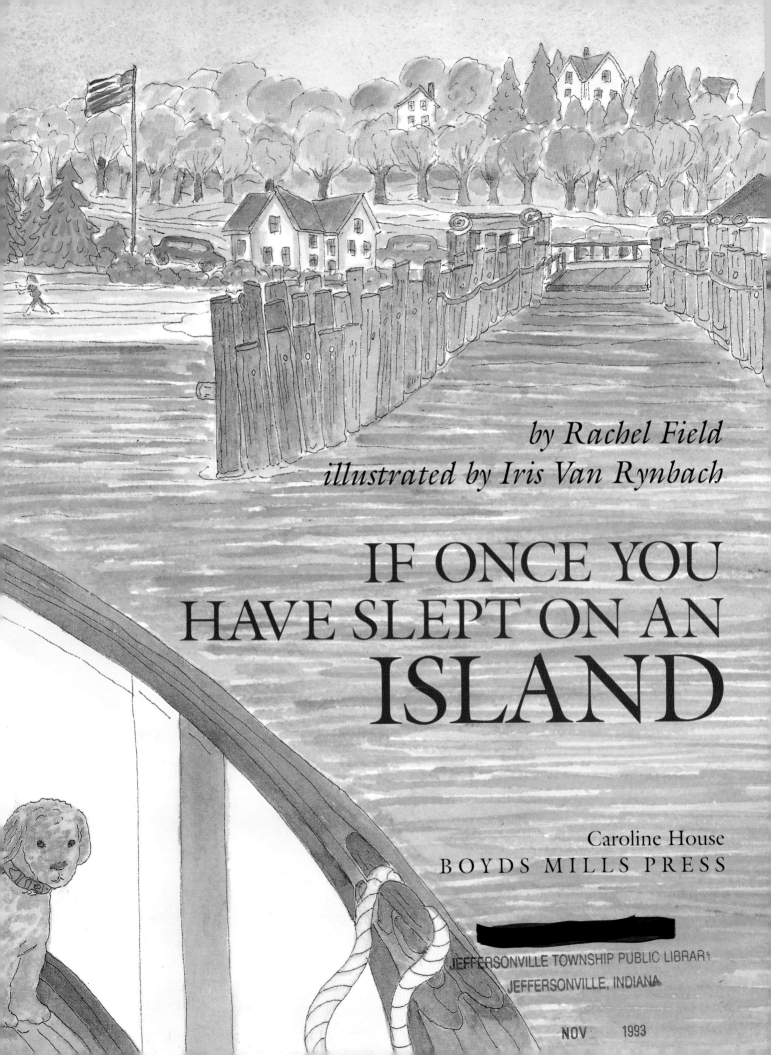

by Rachel Field
illustrated by Iris Van Rynbach

IF ONCE YOU
HAVE SLEPT ON AN
ISLAND

Caroline House
BOYDS MILLS PRESS

"If Once You Have Slept on an Island," copyright 1926 by The Century Company, from TAXIS AND TOADSTOOLS by Rachel Field. Used by permission of Doubleday, a division of Bantam Doubleday Dell Publishing Group, Inc.

Illustrations copyright © 1993 by Iris Van Rynbach
All rights reserved
Published by Caroline House
Boyds Mills Press, Inc.
A Highlights Company
910 Church Street
Honesdale, Pennsylvania 18431

Publisher Cataloging-in-Publication Data
Field, Rachel, 1894-1942.
If once you have slept on an island / by Rachel Field ; illustrated by Iris Van Rynbach.—1st ed.
[32] p. : col. ill. ; cm.
Summary: Poem describes the change one will experience after sleeping on an island.
ISBN 1-56397-106-2
1. Islands—Juvenile poetry. 2. Children's poetry, American.
[1. Islands—poetry. 2. American poetry.] I. Van Rynbach, Iris, ill. II. Title.
811.54—dc20   1993
Library of Congress Catalog Card Number: 92-71271

First edition, 1993
The text of this book is set in 24-point Galliard Roman.
The illustrations are done in watercolors.
Distributed by St. Martin's Press
Printed in Hong Kong
10 9 8 7 6 5 4 3 2 1

To my father,
with thanks for all
the Shelter Island summers.
—I.V.R.

If once you have slept on an island
You'll never be quite the same;

You may look as you looked the day before

And go by the same old name,

You may bustle about in street and shop;

You may sit at home and sew,

But you'll see blue water and wheeling gulls

Wherever your feet may go.

You may chat with the neighbors of this and that

And close to your fire keep,

But you'll hear ship whistle and lighthouse bell

And tides beat through your sleep.

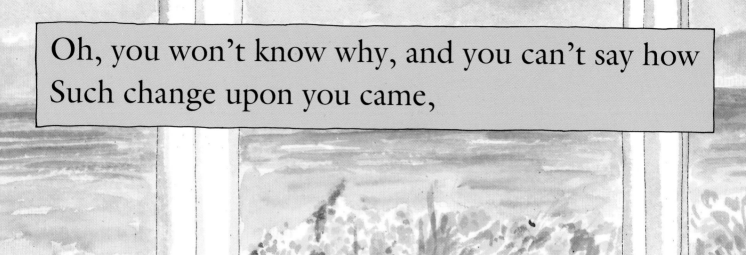

Oh, you won't know why, and you can't say how
Such change upon you came,

But—once you have slept on an island

You'll never be quite the same!